# WHO'S TALKING?

Other Woodside School Stories are:

1 THE FRIGHT 1

3 LOUD MOUTH 3

4 SOPPY BIRTHDAY 4

5 KING OF SPUDS 5

6 WHO'S FOR THE ZOO? 6

A WOODSIDE SCHOOL STORY

# WHO'S TALKING?

Jean Ure

Illustrated by
Susan Hellard

ORCHARD BOOKS

ORCHARD BOOKS
96 Leonard Street, London EC2A 4RH
*Orchard Books Australia*
14 Mars Road, Lane Cove, NSW 2066
ISBN 1 85213 659 6
First published in Great Britain 1988
First paperback publication 1994
Text copyright © Jean Ure 1988
Illustrations copyright © Susan Hellard 1994
Printed and bound in Great Britain
A CIP catalogue record for this book is available from
the British Library.

# Contents

## Chapter 1

"Who's talking?" Miss Lilly looked up, sharply. Her eyes raked the class. "Sophie? Is it you?"

"Me?" said Sophie.

She opened her eyes wide, trying to look innocent. Her eyes were quite wide to begin with. She was a bouncy, merry-faced girl with glossy black curls, an infectious grin, and mouth that never stopped talking. Miss Lilly, when she was in a good mood, called her 'mouth-on-a-stick'.

Today Miss Lilly was in a bad mood. When she was in a good mood she didn't mind a bit of chatter (so long as it didn't turn into a hubbub). Today she had told them to "get on with your maths cards—and do it, please, without noise."

But Sophie hadn't *been* making a noise. All she'd been doing was just whispering. It wasn't fair!

"I don't want to hear another word," said Miss Lilly, "from you or anyone else, for at least half an hour."

Sophie sighed and twisted a strand of hair round her finger. Maths cards were so *boring*. Anything was boring that meant you had to sit at a desk and not talk. Sophie's card that she was working on was all about being at a funfair. She had £5 to spend and she had to work out what to spend it on. The Dodgems, the Whirligig, the Zigzag...she wished she *was* at a funfair. Anything rather than maths cards. There was another forty minutes to go before the bell rang for break.

In three weeks' time she was having a party. Three weeks seemed ages to wait, but her mother had said she must start sending out invitations this weekend. She wondered who she would send them to. The Gang, obviously. (The Gang were the Spider Gang—Alison Webb, known as Spider; Shirin Shah and Colette Goodchild,

known as Shiri and Col; and, of course, Sophie herself. Sophie was known as Soapsuds, or Soapy.)

Who else would she send an invitation to? Cameron Philips, *maybe*; if he promised to behave himself and not start a fight. Last term when Col had invited him and the rest of the Zombies (the Zombies were Cameron's gang) to her birthday party, they had all got together in the middle of the floor and begun punching and kicking for absolutely no reason at all.

10

Colette's mum had been ever so angry. She had said if that was the way Colette's friends behaved, then she wasn't ever going to let her have any more parties ever again. Maybe Sophie wouldn't bother inviting Cameron.

She turned to look at the girls. She wasn't inviting Leonie Shanks; Leonie Shanks was just a show-off. Pavindra Patel wasn't bad, but she was never allowed to go anywhere even when she was invited. Jackie-Lee Gibbs was OK; she'd invite Jackie.

Then there was Soozie Schuster, who had been new that term.

Soozie was nutty as a fruit cake. Sophie quite liked her, even though Shiri and Spider said she was a fright.

They were just jealous, because Soozie could pull faces and make people laugh. She could even make that little mousy Onslow giggle. In fact, Catherine Onslow had quite come out of her shell since becoming friends with Soozie. Maybe she would invite both of them and never mind if Shiri and Spider *did* grumble.

"Oy!" Sophie leaned out of her desk to

poke at Colette with the tip of her ruler. Colette was the only one of the Gang within reach. Last term they had all sat together, but this term Miss Lilly had separated them because she said they talked too much. It was ever so unfair.

Colette twisted round.

"What d'you want?"

"You know my party that I'm having?"

"What about it?"

"Shall I ask *them*?"

"Them?"

"*Them*."

"What, to your—"

13

"Sophie!" Miss Lilly rapped with her pencil on Nicky Edwards' desk lid. (Nicky, who was a bit of a clown, clutched at his arm, pretending he had been shot.) "How many times do I have to tell you? I will not put up with this constant chitter-chat! If you can't be trusted to get on with your work, you'd better change places...come over here and sit next to Pavindra. Lucy, you can go and sit in Sophie's place. And you can stay like that for the rest of term."

It was so unfair! Sophie gathered up her books and set off, pouting, across the room. She would be miles away from anybody now. Why was Miss Lilly so mean? She wasn't the only one who talked. Some people did worse things than just talking. Suzanne and Catherine *giggled*, and they were allowed to sit together.

Resentfully, she settled into her place next to Pavindra. Pavindra, who was doing what she was supposed to be doing, which was working on the maths card, looked up and smiled, rather shyly. Sophie smiled back. Pavindra was all right; she hadn't got anything against Pavindra. It was Miss Lilly, being beastly and having favourites. She never told Nicky Edwards off, and he was quite the naughtiest boy in the whole class.

She wondered if she would invite Nicky Edwards to her party.

Sophie opened her exercise book at the middle pages and began to make out a list: Spider, Shiri, Col...

Pavindra, at her side, had gone back to her maths card. Sophie pulled a face: Pavindra was so *good*. She worked harder than absolutely anybody. When they had tests she always came top—well, practically always. Last week Catherine Onslow had come top and Pavindra had only come second. Pavindra had been really upset. She hadn't said anything—Pavindra hardly ever did say anything, she was quite the opposite to Sophie—but you could tell that it was something she hadn't been expecting. Sophie had felt quite sorry for her. It obviously meant a lot to Pavindra, coming top.

Pavindra flicked her plaits over her shoulders as she turned to the next card. Heavens! She had almost done the lot! Sophie had only done one. Maths was so *boring*. She wondered whether Pavindra actually enjoyed it or if she were just naturally hard-working.

Pavindra never got told off for talking or making a noise or not paying attention. Normally, Sophie would have hated anyone as goody-goody as that, but you couldn't hate Pavindra, she was always so polite and so helpful. It was a pity she didn't come to parties. Somebody had said that it was because of her parents, because they were so strict. But you'd think even the strictest of parents would make an exception just *once*.

Sophie leaned across the desk.

"Hey, Pavindra! If I asked you t—"

"Sophie Waters, you are talking yet again!" This time, Miss Lilly didn't just rap with her pencil, she brought the flat of her hand down, *slap*, on the desk. She was plainly very angry. Her cheeks, which were usually quite pale (which was why some of the boys called her Lilly White) had developed two little scarlet patches, and her lips were all scrunched up with crossness. "Sophie, I am getting very tired of you!  I shall not warn you again…if I catch you talking once more, just *once more*, there will be trouble. Do I make myself clear?"

Sophie nodded. "Yes, miss."

"Very well, then! Now get on with your work."

Sophie did so. Life was ever so unfair.

## Chapter 2

Next morning, Miss Lilly wasn't there. Mrs Kenny, the school secretary, told them that she had the flu. Sophie thought that it served her right. People that picked on people *deserved* to get the flu. She jolly well hoped she had it for weeks and weeks.

By the end of the morning, she wasn't so sure that she did hope Miss Lilly had the flu for weeks and weeks...a supply teacher had come to take her place. Sometimes supply teachers were quite nice; you could giggle and talk and flick paper and they

didn't mind a bit. This one was absolutely horrible. Her name was Miss Mickleberg and she had black hair all scragged back, and thin, mean lips that went into a straight line.

All the time she was taking the attendance register she kept stopping and looking at people with her eyes narrowed. One of the people she looked at was Cameron Philips; another was Nicky Edwards. When she got to Sophie she didn't just look, she said, "You're the talker! I shall be watching out for you."

Sophie didn't say a word for the rest of the day.

The following morning, Miss Mickleberg was still there. All the class were complaining about her, saying how horrid she was. Kelly Flanagan said that her sister Tracey, who was in Class 6, had a friend called Debra Kyte who knew someone who went to a school where Miss Mickleberg had been deputy head.

According to Kelly, according to Tracey, according to this person that Debra Kyte knew, if Miss Mickleberg didn't like people she used to shut them away in the stationery cupboard. She used to leave them there for hours and hours. Once she had left a girl there for so long that she had died and become a skeleton.

Sophie wasn't too sure that she believed the bit about the skeleton—because surely somebody would have have wanted some stationery long before that?—but she could quite believe that Miss Mickleberg would shut people into cupboards.

"Probably leaves them there till dead of night then goes back to suck their blood." That was Colette, who had a thing about vampires. She thought that practically everybody was one.

"Prob'ly hacks 'em with a knife!" said Ben Morrison. Ben Morrison was one of the Zombies: the Zombies liked to talk of people doing things that were violent.

Sophie didn't really believe in vampires, and she didn't think (probably) that Miss Mickleberg would go so far as to hack people, but she did agree with Colette that it would be "best to be on the safe side...don't want to do anything that might set her off."

25

After assembly Miss Mickleberg announced that they were going to have tests. They were going to have tests for spelling, and arithmetic, and history, and geography, and just about everything that you could think of. They were going to spend the whole day at it. She wanted to find out, she said, how they compared with other schools she had taught in.

The class sat stunned, mouths agape in disbelief. Tests all day? They would never survive! Cameron Philips, bolder than the rest, stuck up a hand.

"We never do tests all day, miss!"

Miss Mickleberg looked at him across the room. Everybody quaked, as they thought of Debra Kyte and the stationery cupboard.

"In that case," said Miss Mickleberg, "today will be something different."

Sophie looked at Pavindra. Pavindra seemed worried. Goodness knows why, since she always came out top.

"We shall start with geography," said Miss Mickelberg. "I shall write up the names of the towns, and you will write down the countries where those towns are to be found. And please remember—" she fixed her gaze upon Sophie—"this is a test. That means there is to be *no talking*. Do I make myself clear?"

Sophie said, "Yes miss."

"Very well, then! Let us begin."

27

Soon there was total silence, broken only by the squeaking of Miss Mickleberg's chalk on the blackboard and the occasional creak of a desk or chair. Not even Soozie Schuster dared make jokes with Miss Mickleberg there. Even Cameron Philips was keeping quiet—even Nicky Edwards had picked up his pen. (He wasn't actually writing with it, but then nobody was quite sure whether Nicky Edwards *could* write.)

Towns, as least, were better than sums. Sophie was quite good at towns. The first was Milan. That was easy: that was Italy. Montreal, that was Canada. Leningrad, Russia. Brussels—

Sophie worked her way steadily down the list. She was just debating whether Madras was in Spain or India when Pavindra leaned across and whispered, "Where is Antwerp?" Sophie was so

surprised that she just sat and stared. Pavindra, asking *her*? *Pavindra*, not knowing?

"Antwerp," whispered Pavindra. She sounded desperate. "Where is it?"

Sophie was just about to write down Belgium and show it to her—because what did it matter, really—when Miss Mickleberg's voice rang out: "Sophie Waters! You are talking!"

"I'm not!" said Sophie. She was indignant: it was bad enough to be accused of it when you were. But when you weren't—

"Do not try and wriggle out of it!" snapped Miss Mickelberg, still writing up towns on the blackboard. "I heard you!"

"You couldn't have!" said Sophie. "Cos I wasn't!"

She waited for Pavindra to own up—say, "Please miss, it was me"—but Pavindra

didn't say anything at all; just bent her
head over her books so that her plaits fell
forward and hid her face.

Slowly and deliberately, Miss
Mickleberg turned from the board. Her
lips had gone so thin they had almost disappeared.

"I do not like little girls who talk behind my back," said Miss Mickleberg. "I do not like little girls who cheat, and I *do not like little girls who tell lies*!"

There was a long and dreadful silence.

"You can go and stand outside the door," said Miss Mickleberg.

Standing outside the door was almost worse than being shut in the stationery cupboard. At least if you were shut in the stationery cupboard there wouldn't be any chance of Mrs Dobie seeing you.

Mrs Dobie was the Head Teacher and last term she had seen Sophie standing outside the door no less than three times. One time it had been for talking, and one time for being cheeky, and one time for creating a disturbance. It had never been for cheating—it had never been for lying. Sophie's cheeks burned. Nobody would ever believe that it hadn't been her! Why didn't Pavindra say something?

It was so unfair!

## Chapter 3

When the bell rang for break and people began coming out of the classroom Sophie decided that she would stop Pavindra and say to her, "Why didn't you own up?" But before she could do so Miss Mickleberg had appeared. Miss Mickleberg said, "You can think yourself lucky that I am not reporting you. Next time, I give you due warning, you go straight to Mrs Dobie!"

Out of the corner of her eye, while Miss Mickleberg was speaking, Sophie saw

Pavindra slip out of the classroom and steal away down the corridor. When she went to look for her in the playground, she wasn't there.

Sophie was determined to find Pavindra. She went down to the cloakrooms and tried all the doors of the lavatories, one by one, rattling the locks and calling out, "Pavindra! Is that you?" From behind most of the doors voices called out, "No, it's not!" or "Shove off!" From behind just one of the doors there was silence. She tried kicking at it, but it was very firmly locked.

"Pavindra?" shouted Sophie. "I know you're there! Why don't you answer me?"

No reply. Furious, Sophie hammered on the door with her fists.

"You just wait, Pavindra Patel! I'll get you for this! If you're not out of there by the time I've counted ten—"

Slowly, the door opened just a crack. A face peered out. The face had freckles and round blue eyes with sandy lashes: it belonged to a tiny child called Rhoda Robinson in Class 3.

"Why didn't you *say*?" snapped Sophie.

Pavindra wasn't in the cloakrooms; she wasn't in the playground; she didn't seem to be anywhere. Yet when the bell rang for the end of the break she suddenly appeared, silent as a shadow, and slipped into line along with the rest. She must have been hiding behind the bicycle sheds or in the corner by the waste bins. Sophie would remember, next time, to look in those two places.

For the rest of the morning they had tests: a history test, an arithmetic test, a spelling test. In the afternoon they were going to have a general knowledge test, and then at the end of the day the results were going to be read out. Miss Mickleberg said that as Sophie had cheated in her geography test she would be given no marks at all for it. Sophie glared very hard at Pavindra, but Pavindra just kept her head bent and said nothing.

At dinner time Pavindra went home — well, not exactly *home*. Her father owned a chemist's shop in the High Street, and Pavindra always went to the shop for her dinner. She went off the minute the bell rang at twelve o'clock and she returned promptly on the dot of one, usually accompanied by her father. It wasn't any use trying to get her at dinner time. But she was jolly well going to get her later!

Sophie tried explaining to the others, as they ate their macaroni cheese (the macaroni cheese looked like horrible yellow snot) that it had been Pavindra who was talking and not her, but of course they didn't believe her. She had known they wouldn't. Colette giggled and said, "Ho ha!" and Alison said, "A likely tale, I *don't* think." Shirin just smiled in her superior way and didn't say anything.

After dinner they had the general knowledge test, which went on for what seemed like hours, right up until the afternoon break. During the break, Pavindra disappeared again. Sophie hunted high and low. She looked behind the bicycle sheds, she looked in the corner by the waste bins, she banged on all the lavatory doors, but she couldn't find her anywhere. Yet when the bell rang for class she came flitting back again, silently out of nowhere, just as she had before. Sophie mouthed at her, angrily, but Pavindra pretended not to notice.

Miss Mickleberg, by now, had finished marking the general knowledge tests. She had added up all the results and was going to read them out, starting at the bottom. Nicky Edwards was bottom: he always was. He just didn't seem to care. Sophie was next, on account of not being allowed to score any marks in the geography test.

Sophie's fists clenched, underneath the desk: she was going to get Pavindra. The horrible cheating cow would come top, as usual, and nobody would ever know that she had tried to pick Sophie's brains to get there. She probably always did pick people's brains. She probably *always* cheated. Imagine coming top by always cheating!

"Fifth," said Miss Mickleberg, "Alison Webb. Fourth, Pavindra Patel. Third—"

Shock waves ran round the class. They hardly bothered listening to who had come third. They were too busy craning to stare at Pavindra. Pavindra *never* came as low as fourth! Something must have gone wrong—Miss Mickleberg must have made a mistake. She must have got her muddled up with someone else.

Serve her right, thought Sophie. Serve her jolly well right.

At going-home time, Sophie hung around after the others had gone, waiting to catch Pavindra as she came out. She knew Pavindra couldn't have gone yet, because when Sophie had left the cloak-room her raincoat had still been hanging there on its peg; and she had to come through the gate, because it was the only way out.

Pavindra appeared at last, walking very quickly, in little nervous steps, casting anxious glances all around. She was obviously half expecting Sophie to be lying in wait — but that didn't stop her jumping as Sophie sprang out.

"You mean pig!" shrilled Sophie. "Why didn't you own up?"

Pavindra gave her a scared look, but said nothing. Sophie stamped a foot.

"What's the matter with you? Have you

gone deaf or something? I asked you a question! Why don't you answer it?"

Suddenly, without any warning, Pavindra turned, ducked under Sophie's outstretched arm and ran.

"You horrible rotten cheat!" shrieked Sophie. "I'll get you for this, you see if I don't! I'll set the Zombies on you, I'll get them to bash you, I'll—"

"*Sophie Waters*," said an awful voice, "*whatever do you think you are doing?*"

## Chapter 4

"You are quite the nastiest, roughest, most ill-behaved child I have ever taught," said Miss Mickleberg. "And one thing I will not tolerate is bullying! First thing tomorrow morning I am reporting you to Mrs Dobie. We shall see what *she* has to say!"

Sophie worried about it all the way home. When she got in, she told her mother.

"She said that I was talking, and I wasn't!"

"That makes a change," said Mrs Waters.

"But it isn't fair!" cried Sophie.

"Oh, I wouldn't say that," said Mrs Waters. She sounded quite cheerful about it. "After all, if you weren't talking this time, you probably were last time. We only get what we deserve."

It still wasn't fair! She still thought Pavindra had behaved as mean as mean could be.

Pavindra wasn't there next morning. Sophie thought at first that she was hiding, but then the bell rang for assembly and she still didn't appear. Too frightened, probably. Serve her jolly well right!

Immediately after assembly Mrs Kenny beckoned to Sophie and said that she was to come with her to see Mrs Dobie. Everyone stared, and wondered what she had done. Only Sophie knew. But it wasn't fair! It was all Pavindra's fault.

On trembly legs, Sophie followed Mrs Kenny up the passage. Mrs Kenny knocked on the door of Mrs Dobie's room.

"Come in!" called Mrs Dobie, in her deep, throaty voice.

Mrs Kenny opened the door. "In you go," she said.

She gave Sophie a little push. Sophie's knee caps began to jiggle. She had thought that Mrs Dobie would be alone, but she wasn't: her room was full of people. There was Pavindra's father, looking very stern; a pretty Indian lady in a sari; and a lady police officer. They all turned their heads to look as Sophie came in.

"This is Sophie," said Mrs Dobie. She crooked a finger at Sophie. "Come and sit down, Sophie. Don't be frightened. These are Pavindra's parents, Mr and Mrs Patel, and this is Policewoman Andrews. We just want to ask you a few questions...it seems that after leaving school yesterday afternoon Pavindra didn't go home. She hasn't been back all night. Nobody knows where she is, and as you can imagine we're all very worried. Now, according to Miss Mickleberg, she saw you talking to Pavindra—"

"Bullying her!" said Pavindra's father.

Mrs Dobie frowned, slightly. Sophie grew pink.

"—talking to her," said Mrs Dobie, "as you came out of school. Is that right?"

Before Sophie could say anything, Pavindra's father had burst out: "The teacher said the child was bullying her! Threatening to get her—to bash her! That is what she said!"

"*Were* you, Sophie?" said Mrs Dobie.

"I didn't mean it!" said Sophie. Her pinkness, by now, had grown to bright redness. She wasn't quite telling the truth, because at the time she *had* meant it. Of course, she wouldn't really bash anyone, not even Pavindra, but just for a moment she had wanted to.

"You see? My child is bullied and this is why she runs away!"

Mrs Patel started saying something, very quietly, in a language that Sophie couldn't understand; but angrily, in the same language, Mr Patel shouted at her and she stopped. The police lady leaned forward.

"Can I ask you something, Sophie? Can

I ask *why* you were threatening to bash
Pavindra?"

"I wouldn't really have bashed her," said
Sophie, "I mean...not really!"

Mr Patel opened his mouth to interrupt,
but Mrs Dobie held up her hand, just as if
he were one of her pupils, and he made an
impatient clicking noise with his tongue
and thumped his fist on the corner of the
desk.

"Tell us about it," said the police lady.

So Sophie told them; all about the geography test, and Miss Mickleberg accusing Sophie of cheating, and how it hadn't been her but Pavindra, and—

"That is not true!" shouted Mr Patel. "My daughter has no need to cheat! She comes top all the time! Why should she cheat?"

Again Mrs Patel started to say something: again Mr Patel shouted her down.

"If I thought that Pavindra was cheating—"

He raised his hand, in a threatening gesture. Sophie flinched, even though she knew he wasn't going to hit her.

"Of course, we haven't yet established," said the police lady, "that anybody actually *did* cheat...maybe Miss Mickleberg just thought that they did, because she heard someone talking. But maybe they were talking about something quite different—nothing to do with the geography test."

Everybody swivelled round to look at Sophie. Sophie looked at Mr Patel. Then she looked at Mrs Patel. Then she looked at the police lady; and lastly at Mrs Dobie.

"Well, Sophie?" said Mrs Dobie. She said it gravely. "Only you can tell us...was Pavindra asking you about the geography test? Or was it something different?"

"Yes," said Sophie.

"Something different?"

Sophie took a breath—and nodded.

"There!" Mr Patel thumped again on the desk, triumphantly. "What did I tell you? What did I—"

This time it was Mr Patel who was interrupted—by the ringing of the telephone on Mrs Dobie's desk. Mrs Dobie said, "Excuse me," and picked up the receiver.

"Yes, Mrs Kenny. What is it?" She listened a moment. "Oh, that's wonderful news!" she said. She turned and beamed at Mr and Mrs Patel. "Pavindra has turned up at her brother's! He's just rung through to let us know — in fact, he's on the line now. Would you like to have a word with him?"

She held out the receiver. Sophie was rather surprised that it was Mrs Patel who took it. She had already come to the conclusion that Mr Patel never let Mrs Patel do anything.

After speaking for a few moments in her own language Mrs Patel said, "Pavindra?" and Sophie guessed, although she couldn't understand what was being said, that Pavindra had come to the telephone. Mr Patel leaned forward, very earnestly, to Sophie.

"Pavindra is a good girl," he said. "She would never cheat."

"No," said Sophie.

"She has no need, you see; because she always comes top. She is a good girl. She works very hard."

"I wonder," murmured Mrs Dobie, "if perhaps she works a little *too* hard?"

Such an idea had obviously never occurred to Mr Patel; just for a moment he looked quite shocked. Sophie might almost have giggled if the occasion hadn't been so solemn. Then, to her confusion,

 Mrs Patel suddenly held out the telephone and said, "Sophie, here is Pavindra. Will you speak to her, please? There is something, I think, that she would like to say to you."

"To me?" said Sophie. Awkwardly, she pressed the receiver to her ear. "Hallo," she said. "This is Sophie."

"I am very sorry I didn't own up," said Pavindra.

"Oh!" All Sophie's redness came rushing back again. "That's all right." She coiled the telephone wire round her finger. "Doesn't matter."

There was a silence; and then, because she didn't know what else to say, she said, "Would you like to come to my party that I'm having?"

Pavindra hesitated. It was Mrs Patel who answered.

"Yes," she said. She looked challengingly at Mr Patel. "Pavindra would like very much to come to your party."

Mr Patel didn't say anything.

## Chapter 5

On Monday morning both Miss Lilly and Pavindra were back at school. Everyone was terribly relieved to see Miss Lilly, but not many people noticed Pavindra. Nobody except Sophie knew that she had run off and gone all the way up to Birmingham to see her brother. Mrs Dobie had warned Sophie not to tell anyone, though Sophie wouldn't have done, anyway.

"So what has been happening while I've been away?" said Miss Lilly. "Anything exciting?"

A chorus of voices hastened to inform her.

"It's been horrible, miss! We've been having tests."

"Yeah, we had this supply teacher—"

"Miss *Milk*bottle."

"She was ever so strict!"

"I'm very glad to hear it," said Miss Lilly. "Perhaps now you'll be better behaved! Let's see what impression she's made on you...just take out your reading

books and see if you can all be very good and quiet for a few minutes while I catch up on things."

Sophie had already finished her book last week with Miss Mickleberg. She flipped through the pages, but it was boring, reading it again. She leaned across and began whispering at Pavindra.

"You are going to come to my party, aren't you? I'll send you a proper invitation. I—"

"Sophie Waters!" Miss Lilly sounded outraged. "This is unbelieveable! You're talking again!"

"Please, miss—" Pavindra's hand wavered into the air. "It wasn't Sophie, it was me."

"Oh! Was it?" Miss Lilly pursed her lips. "Very well, so this time it was somebody else. But next time—" she nodded at Sophie. "Just be warned. Next time there'll be trouble!"

Talk about un*fair*.